This
PJ BOOK
belongs to

_____

_____

*'To Alex and Judah, the new readers, here's something
to read with granddad Peter.'*
Shoham

'For Sammy and Jack.'
Michael

Green
Bean
Books

First published in the UK in 2019 by Green Bean Books
c/o Pen & Sword Books Ltd
47 Church Street, Barnsley, S. Yorkshire, S70 2AS
www.greenbeanbooks.com

Text © Shoham Smith 2013
Illustrations © Vali Mintzi 2012
Copyright © Kinneret, Zmora-Bitan, Dvir Publishing House Ltd 2013
English edition © Green Bean Books 2019
English translation rights arranged through S.B.Rights Agency – Stephanie Barrouillet

Hardback ISBN 978-1-78438-377-0
Paperback ISBN 978-1-78438-419-7

Designed by Tina García
Edited by Claire Berliner and Kate Baker

Printed in China by 1010 Printing International Ltd
061932.8K1/B1411/A7

SIGNS in the WELL

"If we think that what is not seen does not exist, it is because our knowledge is very limited."

Michel de Montaigne
Masses (Book 2, Chapter 2)

Translations from the illustrations

Page 22 But the mountain falling comes to dust and the rock is moved from its place.

Page 23 Water wears away the stones.

Page 25 Water wears away the stones. Water wears away the stones. Water wears away the stones.

Page 29 Love your neighbour as yourself. *This is the most important rule in the Torah. All is foreseen and freedom of choice is given. The world is judged in goodness, but in accordance to one's good deeds.*

SIGNS *in the* WELL

Written by Shoham Smith
Illustrations by Vali Mintzi
Translated by Annette Appel

Young Akiva was a goat-herd,

experienced and skilled in his work.

He knew how to play beautiful tunes on his shepherd's flute.

He knew how to take care of newborn kids

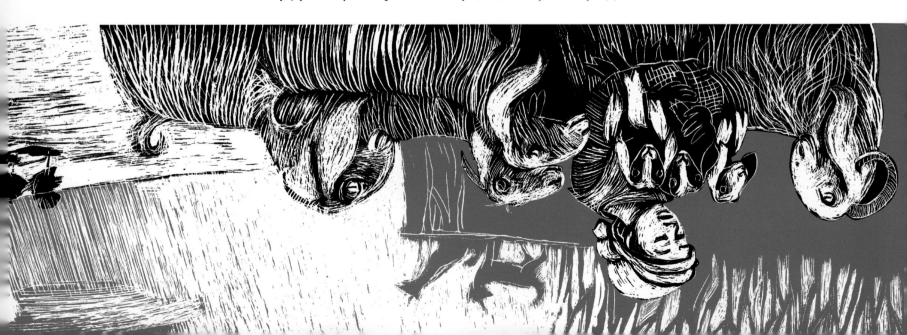

and how to lead the flock over rocky paths.

He never got lost in the hills,
and he knew where the best-tasting grasses grew.

But there was one thing Akiva did not know – he did not know how
to read. His family could not afford to send him to school.
Instead, Akiva helped his father herd the goats.

Akiva felt content. He liked leading the flock through the hills to graze.
He liked caring for the little kids, watching them grow,
and thinking his quiet thoughts.

But sometimes at night, right before he fell asleep, Akiva would think:
If only I knew how to read, then I'd really be happy.

A person who knows how to read can study and become wise.
One day, thought Akiva, *one day I will learn.*

But years passed, and Akiva did not learn how to read.
At the age of forty he still could not decipher the written word.

It's too late now, he thought. *I am too old to learn new things.*
If I started now, I would never succeed.

One day, when Akiva was out herding his flock, he spotted a well.
He hurried over to draw water for his thirsty goats.
As he leaned into the well, he noticed something strange.

This was the first well he'd seen with marks etched in its walls.
How did this happen? thought Akiva. *A person could never have reached
down so far and made marks so deep. Maybe it was an animal?*

Akiva thought and thought but couldn't find an answer. *I will go to the Torah study hall,* he decided. *I'll be sure to find a scholar there who knows the meaning of these signs.*

So Akiva found a scholar who listened to his question.
"It's obvious," the scholar said immediately. "The water in the well penetrated the stone."
"Water can cut into stone?" asked Akiva. "That seems impossible."

"Well, it didn't happen in just one day," answered the scholar,
"but slowly, over a period of many, many years."
"I read the answer in the Bible, the holiest book of our people," said the scholar.

"There it is written: 'Water wears away the stones.'
If you could read, you would know the answer yourself..."
Akiva dropped his head in shame, embarrassed that he was still unable to read.

Akiva returned to the well. He looked closely at the signs in the stone and chanted softly: "Water wears away the stones. Water wears away the stones!" Suddenly, his eyes lit up. The water had worn into the stone, drop by drop!

If I work hard enough, Akiva thought,
letter by letter, I can learn to read. As the water made its mark
in the stones, knowledge will make its mark in my mind.

Akiva began learning, one letter and then another, words and then sentences.
He studied more and more, until finally he could understand difficult and complex texts.
Akiva was an excellent student.

Only a few years later he was a teacher himself and a great rabbi.
Before long he had become very famous and had thousands of students.

At times, while sitting in the Torah study hall, Rabbi Akiva
would gaze out the window at the rolling hills and reminisce
about his days as a shepherd.

He thought to himself, *Today, I am still a kind of shepherd: I have become a leader of my people. I am proof that it's never too late to learn!*